LIES KNIVES AND GIRLS IN RED DRESSES

For my mother (1910–2009).
She read to me and said that someday
I might like to write stories of my own.
R. K.

In loving memory of Gabi Goldner,
who encouraged me to imagine . . .
A. D.

Text copyright © 2012 by Ron Koertge
Illustrations copyright © 2012 by Andrea Dezsö

First edition 2012

Library of Congress Cataloging-in-Publication Data is available.
Library of Congress Catalog Card Number pending
ISBN 978-0-7636-4406-2

RRC 17 16 15 14 13 12
10 9 8 7 6 5 4 3 2 1

Printed in Crawfordsville, IN, U.S.A.

This book was typeset in ThrohandInk.
The illustrations were created digitally.

Candlewick Press
99 Dover Street
Somerville, Massachusetts 02144

visit us at www.candlewick.com

LIES KNIVES AND GIRLS IN RED DRESSES

RON KOERTGE

ILLUSTRATED BY ANDREA DEZSÖ

CANDLEWICK PRESS

Do you want to sleep? Find another storyteller. Do you want to think about the world in a new way?

Come closer. Closer, please.
I want to whisper in your ear.

TABLE OF CONTENTS

THE STEPSISTERS

I write this on a brailler, a kind of typewriter
for the blind. Ella is married and happy. Our
Ever After is silence, darkness, and bitterness.

We have names, by the way. She's Sarah
and I'm Kathy. We were always close.
As girls we lay in bed kissing and pretending
one of us was the prince. We were practicing
for happiness.

Mother turned us against our stepsister,
belittling her. But there was always
something dangerous in those blue eyes,
and we should have seen it. Even in tatters
Ella was desirable — a little thigh showing
here, some soot at her cleavage. And what
a tease — dashing away at midnight leaving
the heir to the throne groaning in his purple
tights.

Then when Mother heard about the big Slipper
Raffle, she never gave up, forcing the surgery
on us. And it almost worked, because
we were on our way to the castle when
those birds warned him. What a scene —

tattletale fowl, blood pouring from our shoes,
Mother howling. And then You-Know-Who
comes out of the kitchen barefoot with some
wisps of golden hair stuck to her brow and he
all but goes to his knees and sucks on her
perfect toes.

And then, insult to injury, we have to go
to the wedding. Mother insisted. There will be
men there. Other princes or earls or rich merchants
or anybody, really, with a penis and a pulse.

Even that wasn't meant to be. As we entered
the church, Ella's vengeful birds plucked out our eyes.
Then nobody wanted us. We were monstrosities,
blind and lame.

So here we are in this deep coffin of sisterhood.
We still hold each other and kiss but now one
of us pretends to be Death and the other his
grateful bride.

RAPUNZEL

A Story in Five Parts

THE HUSBAND: We were getting along fine. I had a good job, the house payments were reasonable. My wife was happy because after trying for months we were finally pregnant. It was interesting to live next door to a witch. We'd sit out with drinks, and scents would waft over the wall. Some bad, but some good, too. Slightly intoxicating. Then one day I came home and my wife was desperate. "I have to have a salad," she cried. "Get some rapunzel from the witch's garden. Please!" So I climbed the wall. I didn't want to, but I did. I thought love would carry me through. Instead, the witch caught me. There I stood with a handful of herbs while she muttered imprecations and a cloud covered the sun. I knew I was in terrible trouble. She glided closer, and her voice was like a saw on stone: "Give me the child your wife is carrying or I'll kill you."

THE WIFE: I've come to understand that I'll always want what I can't have. And if I do get it, something happens. It's karma. It's my burden in this incarnation. Believing this allows me to stay married. I drive to my therapist three times a week. We go over it again: my husband is not a knight or a hero. Just a man with a bald spot and gas. If he'd died in that garden clutching a handful of rapunzel, what good would that have done? I was the witch's surrogate; I carried her child. It was never meant to be mine.

THE WITCH: I couldn't wait for Rapunzel's hair to grow
so it could tumble from the tower like a torrent of gold.
I longed to bury my nose in it. Stand up to my neck in it.
The smell of her made my ears buzz. It was lovely when
we were together. She was curious about everything:
Did I ride a broomstick? Did I have a cat and would I bring
it to see her? Did I know spells for love and health and would
I teach her? I could deny that sweet child nothing. Then he
showed up with his royal scepter. He called to her as I did,
he climbed where I climbed, he lay where I lay, his hands
in all her hair. Well, I showed them. I sent her to a wilderness
and he went out the window. Good riddance.

THE PRINCE: I fell into thorns and survived, but
I was blinded. There were a lot of princes in rehab.
Most of them were just waiting for their fathers
to die and felt guilty. And I came to understand
they all looked alike, so they had identity issues.
And then there was the dolor of Ever After. I
adjusted. My hearing got keener, my sense of
smell and taste more discriminating. When I
found Rapunzel and her tears restored my sight,
I almost died from the shock. All those colors!
By all accounts I'm handsome and happy.
I can wrap myself in golden hair every night
if I want to. But sometimes I go to the window
instead and close my eyes and Rapunzel says,
"Sweetheart, what's wrong?" And, God help me,
I'm not sure I even know myself.

RAPUNZEL: Up there in the tower, I was a catapult
of questions — one after another to keep the witch at bay.
So when I first saw the prince, I was thrilled. I wouldn't
be a prisoner forever after all! But he was so hairy.
His kisses were like blows. His cheeks sanded down
my mother-of-pearl skin and the Plow Horse Game
skinned my knees. I admit he made me feel real.
I was vapor, otherwise, only collecting into the form
of a girl when the witch called and I tugged and she
climbed and she was the oven and I was the bread.
Now that it's all over, I suppose I'm happy. I love
my daughter. But the prince is moody and thinks
of himself. While the witch thought only of me.

THUMBELINA

The Mole's Story

I don't see, but I know things.

Nature does that sometimes — curses and blesses,
takes away and gives. I'm blind but I see.

The toad was Thumbelina's first fiancé.
That was an impossible match. She was Persephone
consigned to darkness and he the Loathsome Bridegroom.

I, on the other hand, let light into my tunnels
for her and have a coat as smooth as velvet.

Her voice was divine, like currants and gooseberries.
Her singing could have drawn ships onto rocks.

All I wanted from her were stories after a long day
of digging. I admit I wanted her all to myself.
Which makes her the girl in the tower and me
the witch. I know that.

Just as I knew the courtship would not end
in marriage. Oh, I went through the motions —
enlarging my den, storing more food,
grooming my fur — because I was curious:
how would I be thwarted?

I knew the end but not the means.
Like humans who know they will die
but not how — microbe or Volvo?
Revolver or respiratory distress?

I lie in the dark and dictate this.
The toad died of a broken heart,
the butterfly Thumbelina tethered
to a lily pad starved to death.

I don't begrudge her happiness, and I understand
how she suffered as an outsider. But the path she took
to find her tiny husband is littered with bodies.

THE LITTLE MATCH GIRL

She's selling CDs on the corner,
fifty cents to any stoner,
any homeboy with a boner.

Sleet and worse — the weather's awful.
Will she live? It's very doubtful.
Life out here is never healthful.

She puts a CD in her Sony.
It's the one about the pony
and a pie with pepperoni

and a mom with warm, clean hands
who doesn't bring home guys from bands
or make some sickening demands.

The cold wind bites like icy snakes.
She tries to move but merely shakes.
Some thief leans down and simply takes.

Her next CD's called *Land of Food*.
No one there can be tattooed
or mumble things that might be crude

and everything to eat is free,
there's always a big Christmas tree
and crystal bowls of potpourri.

She's weak but still she plays one more:
She's on a beach with friends galore.
They scamper down the sandy shore

to watch the towering waves cascade
and marvel at the cute mermaids
who call to her and serenade.

She can't resist. The water's fine.
The rocks are like a kind of shrine.
The foam goes down like scarlet wine.

One cop stands up and says, "She's gone."
The other shakes his head and yawns.
It's barely 10:00, and life goes on.

BEARSKIN

The soldier had seen the devil in the desert.
And he'd seen the devil's toys — IEDs,
VBIEDs, the maniacs with dynamite
strapped to their chests.

So he wasn't surprised when the devil came
right up to him in the VA hospital room and said,
"So here's the deal. If you can wear a bearskin
for seven years, you'll stop having bad dreams.
And I'll make you rich. But if you ever
take the bearskin off, I get your soul."

Why not? Could it be any worse than the two
tours he'd just logged? He had nothing to live
for, anyway. The nights were awful.
He was impotent. His friends were dead.

He wore a fur coat from that day on.
He didn't bathe or shave. He was like a bear.
The doctors couldn't get through to him.
The meds didn't reach him.

An old man who came to see somebody
in the psych ward needed money badly.
He had daughters, debts, and no job.

Every month Bearskin gave him money.
What did he need it for, anyway?

Then the old man's daughters came to
say thanks and recoiled in horror — the look
of him, the odor. But the youngest took
his paw and said, "You're not what you seem.
I'm tired of one boy after another trying
to put his hand under my sweater."
Then she gave him half a ring and kept
the other half.

Now it wasn't so easy to wait, but he did.
Finally, the devil returned and took the coat
and grudgingly shaved him and grudgingly
bathed him and made him rich and gave him
a good night's sleep — free from explosions
and blood.

The soldier looks at himself in the mirror.
Not bad. The Italian suit fits perfectly.
Outside, a fully loaded Porsche sits at the curb.
There's only one place he wants to go.

21

The older sisters make a fuss, pressing
their breasts against him and licking
their lips. Only the youngest is modest,
explaining that she is waiting for
someone special.

"Thank God," he says, showing her his half
of the ring which he'd kept around his neck
with his dog tags.

Frustrated, the other sisters run out
into the street where they are hit
by a bus. The devil snatches their souls
from their bodies like handkerchiefs
as the soldier embraces his bride-to-be.

TWELVE DANCING PRINCESSES

When one sleeps, they all sleep. When one pouts,
they all pout. And they all wear out their shoes
in a roadhouse by the lake.

What's the problem, really?
Not the shoes — Daddy is King Daddy.
He can get more shoes. It's the deception.
Every night he locks them in.
Every morning they show him
the damage and rub his nose in it.

His powerlessness over the tremendous mystery
of daughters. The white milk of the body,
the moonlight white of their teeth.
How in the world do they do it?

Along comes a soldier with a Cloak of Invisibility
that a crone loaned him. Thanks to that,
Sergeant No-Name follows the girls through
the trapdoor in their bedroom, crosses the lake,
and watches them jiggle and cavort.

When he tells the king, the full force
of twelve baleful glances stuns him
even as he ponders his reward:
choose any daughter.

Now they're really mad. They're not doughnuts
in a box, oranges in a sack, pennies in a dish.
They're a force to be reckoned with.

They shove the soldier out the door and remind him
that there's plenty for him to do in other realms:
pushovers in towers, scaredy-cats in forests, wimps
in comas. So skedaddle.

Alone at last, they tattoo one another with spindles
and ink. They serve one another strawberries
and cream. When King Daddy comes to kiss them
good night, they say they're sorry and they promise
never to deceive him again.

But in the morning, their shoes are in tatters.

MEMOIRS OF THE BEAST

I was not merely ugly. I was an animal.
I didn't sit at the table clumsily holding
a fork. I ate by myself in the tall grass,
tearing smaller animals to pieces,
getting my paws damp
with blood.

Every night I asked her to marry me.

I won her over the same way
I hunted — loping after the fawn
I wanted to eat, never in a hurry,
making it a game, tiring her out,
nipping at her heels playfully
until eventually she almost wanted
me to break her neck and open her
up like a purse.

Except, of course, Beauty didn't die.
Her heart opened like a rose.
And her love, I admit,
transformed me.

I rose from the stink and the fur
and was a man again. I took her
hand and almost licked it, then
caught myself and waited until she
kissed me.

*

We're happy now. We're very,
very happy. But I have to admit
there's not much to do in Ever After.
It's always sunny and 78°. Every
night the fireworks light themselves.

*

With a sigh, sometimes, I brush
my perfect teeth and remember when
they were fangs.

HANSEL AND GRETEL

They're not just brother and sister.
They wear each other's clothes. They answer
to either name. They're wedded to each other.
A white wedding — perfect and chaste.

And no wonder. Their parents want to kill them.
Not the father so much, but he's a beaten dog.
A jellyfish, a limp noodle, a nobody.

The first time they're led into the forest,
Hansel's trick with white stones works.
So back they come to the stinking cottage
with its leaning outhouse and crumbling
roof. Their mother is eating rat soup
and she groans when she sees them.

Out they go again, and this time the birds
eat Hansel's trail of crumbs. They're famished
when they reach the gingerbread cottage.

So there's a witch. Their mother is a bitch,
which is worse really. Here there's lots to eat,
a candy bed to cuddle in.

Not that it's perfect. There's that oven and the possible
Hansel-on-a-Stick. So they hold out as long
as they can, fooling the stupid witch with a bone
and lying through their teeth.

They eat and eat, filling up the moist recesses
of their little bodies. Hansel's shed is comfortable.
Gretel visits him at night and they cling to each other.
Neither will ever marry another. They promise to be
brother and sister forever. And murderers.
And thieves.

Next morning, they bake the witch, take the rubies
and gold, and make their way home. They're rich now.
Dad is elated to see them. Sadistic Mom is dead.
Happily Ever After, right?

Not so fast. Regularly the siblings slip out from under
their 400-thread-count sheets and pad into their father's
plush bedroom. They watch him sleep. They fondle
the lockets that carry the witch's ashes. They like
being together, just the two of them. They like revenge.

So they'll all go on a picnic. Dad and the kids.
Back into the forest. Deep, deep. So deep
nobody will ever find him.

GODFATHER DEATH

A man with a dozen children buys Death a beer
and asks him to be his next child's godfather.

Death is flattered. Not many people want to hang out
with him. His ride is that lumbering hearse and he doesn't
wear thousand-dollar suits, just that gruesome hoodie.

So he tells the man, "Your son will be a famous athlete
even in high school. He'll win the Heisman Trophy
as a Trojan, then dominate the pros followed by a career
in broadcasting. He need only listen to me before every
game."

The boy grows up, handsome and popular. He's
being scouted as a tenth grader and goes to USC
on a scholarship. Death comes to him in the locker
room and says, "Make it look close. I like to bet
the under."

The boy is a phenom, then a legend. He's starting
for Miami when a beautiful girl stops him
at a local high-dollar spot. "If you could blow it
wide open for a change, I could afford to pay
for my father's dialysis."

She's not the usual chicken head ho.
She's a swan while the others are sparrows.
She's a field after rain. They're vacant lots.

He wins by forty and Death is outraged. The quarterback
pretends to be sorry, but it's thrilling to disobey Death.
It's the most fun he's had in years: showing Death
who's boss, rubbing Death's nose in it. What does
Death know, anyway? His mama so stupid she thinks
Meow Mix is a dance album for cats.

So it's not the juice he's addicted to. Or the woman.
Or the money. It's this. Next week, he's ahead
by ninety at halftime.

Death snatches him out of his cleats. Underground
are 10 million candles, each one a life. Some are
long and vigorous, others just about to go out. His
is measured in millimeters. "Oh, please, Godfather!"

Death takes a deep breath. "What's the problem,
hotshot? You're going out a winner."

THE UGLY DUCKLING

"Hey! Are you fresh off the boat? Did you just
sneak across the border? Is that your hair
or barbed wire? Are you deaf, too, you
ugly son of a bitch?"

With his iPod all the way up, nothing in this
world can touch him. Just over his pulse
is a fresh tattoo — a dotted line and the words
— — — — — Cut Here — — — — —

Grief is a street he skates down. "Hey,
donkey's ass!" He bides his time, sanding
away his fingerprints, wondering how he
could get all his assailants in one room.

Here a garage, there a squat, beside
the underpass, down by the drainage ditch.
Enough ganja and the trees put their arms
around him as swans emerge

from the angel mist, bow their beautiful
heads and say, "Please don't go away like
that again. We were worried sick."

DIAMONDS AND TOADS

Two sisters. Different, of course. Pretty and not so pretty.
Kind and not so kind. Opposites. Antipodal. Antonyms.

Because one shares her lunch with a fairy, she is rewarded:
every word from her mouth will be a flower or a precious stone.

The other is spiteful and cranky and selfish, so she is punished:
every word from her mouth will be a snake or a toad.

Do you see the ending? Some nice prince gets a slot machine
for a wife. The other marries a herpetologist.

Except it isn't that simple. The gift/curse can't be turned off.
There's no such thing as a casual conversation:

Out come the rubies and pearls. Or the vipers and toads.
Making love means scribbling notes and destroying the mood.

Rueful. Everyone is rueful, the husbands especially.
At first it was fascinating. Later, not so much. And now. Yikes!

The sight of two servant girls gossiping excites those guys
more than the local pornography. They start coming home late.

"Where have you been?" the sisters shriek, covering the floor
with pearls or asps. The men hedge and stammer, then admit,

"All right. We've been listening to somebody else, somebody
who doesn't puke every time she opens her mouth."

Next morning the men are found swollen and disfigured,
with diamonds where their eyes used to be.

THE FROG PRINCE

Sometimes when girls get together, they vow
to just put their dreams away forever
because boys are creeps, sleazes, troglodytes
and toads. They're poisoned apples, and spikes
in the heart. Bulldozers with bad breath,
gangplanks to walk off of, horny, grabby,
promise-breaking bastards.

And yet. Images of Ever After linger on the retina.
Isn't there somebody somewhere sweet as
a flock of lambs? But smarter and taller.

A princess loses a golden ball in a well and a frog
offers to fetch it for her if he can eat from her plate
and sleep on her pillow. Will she give her word?
Sure. But when he emerges from the dark water,
she takes her ball and flees.

That evening, he hops to the castle, demands to enter,
orders flies for his entrée, then wants to go
upstairs. He croaks, "Remember your promise."

In her room he wants the covers turned back. She can
imagine his webbed feet on her yum-yum skin,
that long tongue down her throat. *Splat!* Up against
the wall he goes.

Then from the wet-work a young man rises. He'd been
spellbound. Now he's free. "Beautiful lady,"
he croons, "my gratitude is as deep as the sea."

OMG. He's a gift shop, a lamb kebab with mint,
a solar panel poetry machine with biceps. He's the path
through the dark woods, the light on the page, a postcard
from the castle and a one-way ticket there. He's the most
astounding arrangement of molecules ever!

Just look at those tights! An honest-to-God prince at last.

THE EMPEROR'S NEW CLOTHES

An Afterword

Nobody believed the boy when he said the Emperor
was naked. His subjects admired his new clothes.
Theirs felt thick and heavy and dull.

The scoundrel tailors said that, for a price, they could
make clothes for everyone. Not quite as airy and splendid
as the Emperor's but still gorgeous, as anybody who
wasn't stupid could see.

The lines were around the block. Who didn't want
new clothes? Who wouldn't want to look almost as good
as the Emperor?

"Now nobody has any clothes!" said the boy, who was
sweating in his mud-colored robes.

"Says who?" someone replied. "There are two thousand of us
and one of you. We're the mob. What we say goes.
If you want to be on the outside looking in forever,
just keep talking."

It was a lonely vigil. Everybody called him tattletale,
spoilsport, whistle-blower. And stupid. Really,
really stupid.

So one day he went to the scoundrel tailors.
"For you," they said, "an outfit just like the Emperor's.
Splendid in every way and lighter than air."

"There you go!" said the first citizens who saw him.
"That's the ticket. You look great!"

And the boy hitched up his invisible pants just a little
because they were new and beautiful, and he didn't want them
dragging on the ground.

THE ROBBER BRIDEGROOM

A miller's daughter is invited to her fiancé's house
deep in the woods.

She barely knows this guy. Her father just wants
her out of the house and off his hands. So when
the trail her husband-to-be leaves for her is
ashes, she begins to get nervous.

Whatever happened to white stones, tulips,
or candy hearts?

Once there, a friendly crone warns her and hides
her and, sure enough, her fiancé and some other
fiends return with a dead girl and argue about
who gets to eat her toes.

Then to get to her wedding ring, they chop off
a finger, and it flies through the air like a carrot
on a cooking show and lands right in
the heroine's cleavage.

If it weren't a finger, that could show up on
America's Funniest Home Videos.

The crone distracts the ghouls with some
drugged wine and soon leads the bride-to-be
out, tiptoeing over the snoring monsters.

She's safe, but what about the other girls
in the village, the ones she went to school
with. She'd slept over at their hovels.
They'd gone shopping at Mall o' the Woods.

So the miller's daughter has a rehearsal dinner.
Her fiancé is on his best behavior, merely
eating goldfish out of the bowl when
no one is looking.

But he starts getting nervous when his beloved
(Oh, her skin is white as Wonder bread,
her little breasts like cupcakes!) relates
a dream about a house in the woods and a band
of miscreants. His face turns red as Mars.
He stutters, "My d-d-d-deliciousness,
it was just a dream."

At which point the miller's daughter pulls
the finger from her bodice and her fiancé
bolts from the table.

He's caught and dismembered by the men
whose wives he has devoured. They're
grateful to the miller's daughter and they
all want to marry her.

But she finds men untrustworthy now. She prefers
to live alone and teach Feminist Theory & Practice
at the local community college.

RUMPELSTILTSKIN

So the first guy says his daughter can milk
twelve cows in one minute. And the second guy
says his daughter can make soup out of stones.
So the miller — who only stopped by for a beer —
blurts that his daughter can spin straw into gold!

Oh, you dog with a galloping heart! You birdbrain,
you loudmouth — now look. The king has your daughter
locked in a room and it's do or die!

The funny thing is, though, she's excited.
What were her prospects before? Hard labor at the mill,
engaged to a rival miller's son, a million or so anonymous
breaths as the milling goes on. She'd rather die.

So there she sits facing a roomful of straw and the clock
is ticking like a bomb and her heart is beating like a bunny's.
If there was only a way. Just then a funny little man comes
out of nowhere. Straw to gold? No problem. She gives him
a necklace, he spins her a bushel. She gives him a ring,
he spins her a roomful. The king is ecstatic. If she can do it
one more time, he will take her for a wife. So she promises
Mr. Pint-Size that he can have her first child.

She loves being queen. She has armor made and fights beside
her husband. They ride at full speed across the moors.
Danger is her drug of choice. Jeopardy is such a rush.

And then she's pregnant and then there's an heir,
which makes her a superstar.

Whoops! It's you-know-who, and he wants the baby.
The queen sobs piteously on bended knee, so Mr. Minuscule,
who likes a game as much as the queen, relents:
"Guess my name or I'll take the child."

Perfect! Now she's hot. Two days of frantic surmise
and then one of her messengers tips her off. Now she's
got Shorty where she wants him. That night she teases
him right up to the last minute, then says his stupid
name. Rumpelstiltskin is so frustrated that he tears
himself in two. Servants whisk the splayed body away.

For a while, the queen is content. There's the baby
with skin like snow and the golden goblets
and the pomegranate juice and the rocking
and the cooing. But there's always that small fire
just under her collarbone.

She summons the hunters, hard men with callused hands.
She asks, "Isn't there a wolf in the forest with teeth
the better to eat me with?"
"Indeed there is, your majesty, but —"
"No buts. Have someone fetch my red cape.
And tell the king not to wait up."

THE LITTLE, SMALL, WEE BEAR

The great, huge bear is not my father. The middle-sized
bear is not my mother. But because we walk on two legs
and talk, we naturally found each other.

The shambling, shuffling, hibernating, honey-loving,
man-killing bears treat us gingerly and with great
suspicion. We are not human, not animal. I am not
a boy or a beast but somewhere in between.

We live a quiet life in our cottage. We sleep, sit,
and eat oatmeal. Every morning we walk
while our breakfast cools.

Humans usually come for advice about their
health, both of the body and the spirit. The middle-
sized bear knows the forest like the back of her paw.
Her tinctures and potions rarely fail. Sometimes
they only need to be embraced, face-down in our fur,
where they weep like their human hearts will break.

Goldilocks wanted to disrupt our lives, eat
our food, criticize our furniture, and soil our beds
with her human stink.

She was a sign, said the great huge bear, of the End Times.
First arrogant, unruly youth with colored hair, then gay
marriage, earthquakes in diverse places followed by a giant
comet, and finally the Apocalypse!

Goldilocks just sneered, then out the window she went,
scrambling toward the deep part of the forest where
it's dark as a mineshaft.

We watched her go. Those ridiculous locks were
the last thing we saw. Then we heard a scream,
and then nothing.

What could we do? We had repairs to make,
sheets to wash, oatmeal to stir until it
and everything else was just right.

BLUEBEARD

Yes it's blue and Yes it tickles and Yes he's had a lot of wives
and nobody knows what happened to them

but he's fun at the party and omigod that castle!
Blue frescoes, a bathtub of cherries, golden trees
with sapphire leaves,

pearls in rainwater, cranes in a paper cage, a diamond
hummingbird in a real hollyhock

I do! I do! I take thee in weirdness and in health.

And then he's gone and she has the keys to everything
and her friends come. They gallop through the castle,
make out under the harpsichord, and taunt

the penguins while she, Mrs. Bluebeard, goes helter-skelter
right to the forbidden room and there are her predecessors
in   pieces   all   over   the   place
and to make matters worse, the stupid key has blood
on it that won't come off and her friends' faces go
police-chalk white and she's on her own

begging pleading entreating promising she'll be good and never
disobey again but Blue has put on a turban and looms over
her like a cliff and will only give her

seven-and-a-half minutes to pray before some scimitar surgery.
She knows her life is on the line but, believe it
or not, she's never been so excited!

Her husband's a serial killer, and her bodice is wet
with tears, but there's a chance her brothers
will show up like winning lottery numbers.

Which does she want more — her hair wound
in the maniac's hands and her white white throat bared,
or the sound of boots on the marble stairs?

LITTLE THUMB

Forget about Little Thumb. He'll save his brothers then end up
at home with the gold.

Let's think about the ogre's children for a change. They had to
live in the middle of nowhere because every time they moved
into a nice neighborhood

some busybody found Dad's name on the Ogre Page
and the protests started.

And if that wasn't bad enough, along comes Little Thumb
and tricks the ogre into cutting his own daughters' throats.
All seven of them.

Okay, they were ogre children with little gray teeth,
but they were kids! The didn't do anything, not really.
Sure, when they played, they boiled their dolls then cut
them into bite-sized pieces. But that was make-believe.

Everybody says the moral of the story
is that short guys can be cunning
and brave.

But I think the moral is that children pay
for the sins of their parents. Ask anybody
who hates to go home after school.

Ask the girl whose mother is a drunk
and a whore. Ask the boy whose dad
is doing twenty-five to life.

RED RIDING HOOD, HOME AT LAST, TELLS HER MOTHER WHAT HAPPENED

Like, where to even start. So, okay — at the beginning. Right.
So I've got the basket of goodies you gave me for Gram
and I'm remembering what you said about the forest but now
that I'm, like, safe and all, I can tell you I was totally looking
forward to that part. With the wolf and all. I'm into danger,
okay? What? You said to tell you the truth and be, like, frank.
Fine, fine, fine. Do you want to hear this story or not? Good.
So I'm in the woods and I hear footsteps or, like, pawsteps and it's
him. And he talks. I'm thinking, "Nobody at school will believe
this. Wait till Shaunelle hears!" So first he's all into my pretty
this and that, like I haven't heard it all before. What? Where
did I hear that all before? At parties. What planet do you live on?
Do you think we make lanyards in Nikki's basement when her
parents are gone? Anyhow, we chat and he gives me his e-mail
and some more insincere compliments and the next time I see him
he's in Gram's bed and she's, like, inside him! Wait till I tell Amber
that! I am so sick of hearing about how her grandma goes to
Cabo all the time and paraglides and scubas. Those things
are like nothing compared to being swallowed whole. And it
kind of makes me want to know what that's like. What? No, as a
matter of fact, if everybody at my school got swallowed whole I
wouldn't want to. It's lame if everybody does it, Mom. How old
are you, anyway? So I, like, let him, sort of like I let Skylar Tibbs . . .

Fine, fine, fine. Later for that, too. Anyway, it's weird inside a wolf, all hot and moist but no worse than flying coach to Newark, but it's not awful and the wolf goes to sleep and snores so loud it's kind of funny, so Gram and I talk about when Dad lived with us and the noises that came out of him. Gross. Then we hear footsteps and an argument and then — *snip, snip, snip* — we're out! It's this cute woodsman. What? I don't know why he had scissors. I thought of that, too. It's kind of, like, gay because as far as accessories go, scissors don't fit at all with the flannel shirt. But we were safe and really grateful and I listened to a little lecture about stranger danger which was weird because *he's* basically a stranger. Then we ate and I kissed Gram good-bye and the woodsman walked me to the edge of the forest where he said, "Maybe next time you'd like to see my ax." Which would make my English teacher, like, light up because she sees symbols everywhere, but to me it just sounded like a guy who didn't get out much and couldn't afford cable. So is there pizza or something in the freezer because I am starved!

EAST OF THE SUN AND WEST OF THE MOON

In the daytime I was a big, white bear, but at night
I was a prince. Did that make me a bipolar bear?

It all started with a curse. (Doesn't it always?)
Here are the specs: I'm going to be a bear / prince
forever unless a beautiful maiden lives with me for a year
but doesn't look at me while we're in bed together.
One year, and no peeking!

So there we are. Sleeping. Not even first base.
And she can't wait. Out comes the candle. I'm
so handsome she leans to kiss me. Wax falls on my
good shirt, the curse kicks in, and I'm flying.

All of a sudden I'm east of the sun and west of the moon
(which is the middle of the middle of nowhere), and
I have to marry a troll princess with a nose that's
three feet long. Kiss the bride? No way!

But just before the wedding, guess who shows up
thanks to the North Wind and a new GPS?
My Own True Love (MOTL).

Now we've got a chance. Whoever can get the wax out
of my shirt will be my bride. (Don't you just
love a curse with an escape clause?)

As old Elephant Nose bleaches and scrubs, the spots
get bigger and darker. But in the hands of MOTL
the shirt is perfect. Better than new.

My troll fiancée explodes in frustration. MOTL
and I take the treasure and get out of there.

I'm a king now with three kids and a spaniel. I rule
in the daytime, but at night I'm just a dad who puts
the kids to bed.

"Tell us a story," they cry right on cue. "The one about when
you and Mommy met."

So I do. I pull up the covers and kiss their royal cheeks.
I turn down the lamp and begin,

"Once upon a time . . ."

THE PRINCESS AND THE PEA

A Monologue

Have you seen the prince? My God, his hands are big as anvils.
Do you know what that would do to me? Do you? I see him
ogling my breasts and I think, "If you want one of them black
and the other one blue, if those are your favorite colors or something, go ahead and grope. Don't let the screaming bother you."
I had to go to the doctor when wheat fell on me. One wheat. A
stalk. So I can't imagine a wedding. Everybody hugging me. I'll
have handprints all over. And then there's the honeymoon.
Oh, my God. He kissed me once and my lips bled. So forget
about the other. I mean that. Forget it. When I was little, a
butterfly landed on my wrist and I was in a cast for a month.
A puppy licked me and I've still got a scar. The night I showed
up here I was running away from a sadistic bastard who beat me.
With chopsticks, I admit, but it was still awful. I need to talk
to the queen. She's desperate. We can work something out.
Some surrogate arrangement, maybe. A lusty wench from the
kitchen, perhaps, who likes a little rough-and-tumble. We'll
make her rich. She'll keep her mouth shut. I'll stuff pillows
under my gown and pretend to puke in the morning. She'll
have the heir and feed him from those big slaphappy knockers.
Someone will help me hold the baby when it's absolutely
necessary but usually I'll wave from a distance so his wailing
won't hurt my ears.

THE OGRE QUEEN

Sleeping Beauty? Just another narcoleptic with a pretty
face if you ask me. But everybody knows her story:
the curse, the nap that lasts a hundred years, the prince.
Old news. My story is much more interesting.

To begin, King Charming married me for my money.
He knew I was an ogre. Not the ugly kind. The kind
with a taste for children. Yum. He turned a blind eye.
Besides the cash, he wanted an heir. Easy peasy.

I wanted to gobble up my own son, but I made do
with the children of destitute millers and farmers.
They were always leaving their kids in the forest,
anyway. All I had to do was follow the croutons
the little darlings left and then make Sibling Soup
with Fennel.

Prince Charming grew up, of course, so I didn't
want to eat him anymore. We never got along,
not really. He stayed away from the castle. Hunting.
Tell me another one. When he did come home,
his robes were ripe with pheromones. He'd been
doing the nasty with somebody.

I bided my time. At last my husband died. Good
riddance to him. And the prince showed up with
his brand-new family. They looked delicious.
Not droopy old SB with goop in her eyes, but
the other two. My grandchildren. The morsels.

They sat on my lap and told me how everything
and everybody in Mommy's castle slept behind
the wall of briars. Everything. Even the fire.

I loved that, because a fire in me had been sleeping,
too. Waiting for Lollytot on a bed of rice. Tyke
with Sauce Vierge.

Of course that didn't happen. Ogres never win
in fairy tales. I ended up in a pit of vipers. Like
that's a bad thing. Vipers are the pasta of Ogreland.

And I didn't die. I never die. Right now I run
my own consulting firm in Washington, D.C.
I see members of Congress now and then, but
most of my business comes from the Pentagon.

WOLF

Let's get a few things straight. Only a few of us like to
dress up like grandmas and trick little girls. Those who
do belong to what we call the Scarlet Underground.
It's not their fault, so they're tolerated if not embraced.

The rest of us are wolves through and through. We enjoy
the chase, the kill, a nap in the sun on a full stomach.

Our enemy is man with his arrogance and greed.
The woodsman in particular. Destroyer of trees.
Clearer of land. Owner of fire.

While he chops and burns and builds, we terrorize his
wife, surrounding her as she goes for water. We howl
outside his windows half the night, and if that doesn't
drive him away we take him out, leaving just a few
bones so the message is clear:

This is our forest. Perfect before you came.
Perfect again when all your kind is dead.